My Cup Runneth Over

by Edna Abbott
graphics Dearl Abbott

682 Wesley Circle
Avon Park, FL 33825

CONTENTS

Chapter 1: MY CUP RUNNETH OVER   2

    Countin' my Blessings   4
    The Apple of His Eye   5
    Stay Upbeat   6
    Is Your Cup Full?   7
    Enjoy Today   8
    I Wonder   9
    Where God Lives   10
    Heart Song   11
    Wrinkles   12
    All the Same   13
    The Dial of Your Heart   14
    Just Forgive 'em   15
    Doing Your Math   16
    Rocking Chairs   17
    The Cup-Filler   18
    Your Cup   19
    Suspicious Folks   20
    Old Love   21

Chapter 2: THE JOY OF FAMILY AND
              FRIENDS   23

    Bedtime Stories   24
    Forever Friends   26
    Special Moments   27
    Selective Hearing   28
    Choosing Your Friends   29
    Walking the Dog?   30
    Cheer 'em Up   31
    Your Are Special   32
    Just Friends   34
    Bitterness   35
    Flawless   36
    Don't Just Stay At Home   37

Blue Mondays 38
Take Time 40
Just Smile 41
School Days 42

Chapter 3: LOVING GOD'S CREATION 45

If We Could 46
Evening Shadows 47
Our Awesome Creator 48
Our I D 50
Birds 52
Penguins 53
Rhinos 54
The Vet 56
Tree Frogs 58
Storms 59
Flowers Are Special 60
Life's Lemonade 61
Smarts 62
Trees 64
Its Different Now 66
Stuff 67

Chapter 4: ACCORDING TO YOUR FAITH 69

Figuring It Out 70
Behind the Scenes 71
Morning Time 72
God Has a Plan for You 73
Faith 74
Change 76
Methuselah 78
Flower Gardens 80
Always There 82
Smile a Lot 83
Make 'em Happy 84
Cold Winds 85

A Day Brightener   86
Propping Us Up   87

Chapter 5; OUR FATHER IN HEAVEN   89

Asking   90
Fancy Prayers   91
Always At Home   92
Quiet Desperation   94
Both Men Prayed   95
I Love Your Word, O Lord   96
The Sacrifice of Praise   98
Trying Out Stuff   99
Small Prayers   100
I Prayed For You   101
Keepin' In Touch   102
God is Always Listening   103
"on Call'   104
Long Prayers   105
The Listener   106
Refinement   107

Chapter 6: BEING GOD'S HANDS AND   109
            FEET

Dressing Up   110
Leaving Footprints   111
Helping Others   112
Living in Style   114
Brighten Someone's Day   115
Shining for Jesus   116
Getting a Song   117
Happiness   118
Hands   120
Opportunities   122
Comin' in First   123
The Givers   124
Your Greatest Gift   126

What God Likes   127
Smiles Help   128
Face to Face   129
Staying On Top th' Heap   130
Living to the Max   131

Chapter 7: IF ANYONE OPENS THE DOOR   133

Only God   134
Zacchaeus   136
Mary   138
Come, Follow Me   140
Christ Loved Kids   141
Just As You Are   142
Still Speaking   144
My Kitchen Window   146
Jesus, the Greatest   148
Unconditional Love   149
Just: Follow Me   150

Chapter 8: I GO TO PREPARE A PLACE   153
             FOR YOU

Finally Home   154
God Loves Color   156
But When We Get to Heaven   158
Heaven   160
Tears   162
Could It Be ?   163
Not a Millionaire?   164

Dedication

We dedicate this book to the many
missionary friends that we have
known and loved across the years.
We feel they are special people
and we greatly admire them and
the work that they have done and
are still doing.

The joy
of the Lord
is your strength

Nehemiah 8:10

Now to begin . . . . . again

We're back. Hope you are ready for another book and that your cup is full and running over. I have more poems that we hope can give you a bit of joy. Everyone's heart is full of something. Happy are those folks who fill their heart full of love and good stuff.

God has made so many beautiful things for us to enjoy—flowers, birds, diamonds, oceans, animals, and a host of other things. I get great joy in seeing these awesome things and to think this great Creator loves and cares for me! How can it get any better than that?

Although I've lived a lot of years I really don't have any profound advice to give except to live large by loving God with all your heart so you will have a song down deep inside. Remember that what is in your head will creep down into your heart. Don't let others steal your joy by small stuff they say or do. Forgive 'em and love 'em so your cup will overflow.

Edna.

Thou preparest a
table before me
in the presence of my
enemies; thou anointest
my head with oil
my cup runneth over

Psalm 23:5

1

My Cup Runneth Over

Countin' My Blessings

When I count up my blessings
  and see all the stuff I've got
They far outweigh my problems
  and things that I have not.
I find that God is awfully good
  in looking after me
And even overflows my cup
  when I'm tired as can be.

When I think of all my problems
  and count 'em one by one
I make myself feel miserable
  because of what I've done.
My attitude comes from my heart
  and it is mine to choose
If I will keep a happy heart
  or if I'll sing the blues.

It's normal to have bad-hair days
  and times when things are tough
But countin' blessings helps to keep
  your living up to snuff.
So set the dial of your heart
  to thankfulness and praise
Then you'll be living in the pink,
  enjoying all your days.

He will love you and bless you
Deuteronomy 7:13

The Apple of His Eye

I wonder if you realize
How much God cares for you—
He's not a politician,
For what He says is true.
His eyes run to and fro, my friend,
Throughout the whole wide earth
To care for those who follow Him,
No matter place of birth.
I guess it kinda' blows my mind
That God loves us so much
He watches o'er us day and night
And gives His special touch.
If we have given the Lord our heart
We need not fear nor sigh,
For in His Book He tells us
We're the Apple of His Eye.

*Keep me as the apple
of your eye; hide me
in the shadow of your wings
Psalm 17:8*

Stay Upbeat

If you will think on happy stuff
And keep your heart upbeat
You'll be surprised how good you feel
And that is hard to beat.
If you can stay on top th' heap
And smile from day to day
You'd sure cheer up a lot of folks
When you pass by their way.

God recommends a merry heart.
It helps to keep you well
So if you'd live a long, long time
Some stories you could tell
To future generations
When they climb up on your knee
And tell some wide-eyed grandkids
The way things used to be

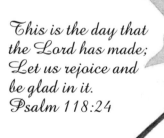

*This is the day that
the Lord has made;
Let us rejoice and
be glad in it.
Psalm 118:24*

Is Your Cup Full?

I wonder if you thank the Lord
   your cup is not on dry
For if it sits on empty
   there must be a reason why.
Some folk get awful busy
   so they fail to keep in touch
With Jesus Christ who died for them
   and loves them very much.

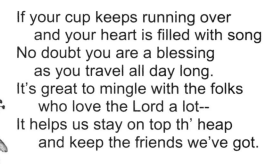

If your cup keeps running over
   and your heart is filled with song
No doubt you are a blessing
   as you travel all day long.
It's great to mingle with the folks
   who love the Lord a lot--
It helps us stay on top th' heap
   and keep the friends we've got.

So count the blessings
   that you have
   and have a glorious day,
It makes God very happy
   if you choose to live that way.
So if your cup runs over
   and your saucer is full, too,
Ask God what you can do for Him.
   He'll tell you what to do.

Taste and see that the Lord is good;
Blessed is the man that takes refuge
in Him. Psalm 34:8

Enjoy Today

Enjoy today.
          It's all you've got.
Just one day at a time.
If you are holding God's big Hand
He'll help with hills you climb.
The Bible says He feeds the birds
So don't just sit and stew
Remember that He loves you much
So keeps His Eyes on you.

So talk to God throughout the day
And hear His joyful sound
And join the other happy folks
Who have what you have found.
God gave us lots of blessings
That He wants us to enjoy,
And best of all He wants to fill
Our hearts with love and joy.

*However many years a man may live;
let him enjoy them all. Ecclesiastes 11:8*

I Wonder . . .

I wonder what you're doing
In your corner of the earth--
Are you sowing seeds of kindness
And doing things of worth?
Do people kinda' seek you out
To pass the time of day
Because they think that you're upbeat
And like the things you say?

If you are loving folks a lot
And living up to snuff
No doubt you are a blessing
To someone whose life is tough.
God needs some happy folks around
To spread a bit of cheer
For good news and encouragement
Are what folks like to hear.

So don't report some gossip
Or don't even criticize
For sometimes what is hearsay
Might be a pack of lies.
If you see someone down and out
Just try to lift him up
And angels might smile down on you
While Jesus fills your cup.

But encourage one another daily
Hebrews 3:13

Where God Lives

God has two places
where He lives--
One's up in Heaven above,
The other place is here on earth
Where hearts are filled with love.
I'm sure that keeps Him busy
Watching over Heaven and all
But He is such an awesome God
He will hear us when we call.

I know folks worship money
And the things that it can buy
But money will not love them back
When life has gone awry.
There's nothing like the touch of God
To help a fella' then
For He knows what has happened
No matter where or when.

So put your hand in God's big hand,
He has good news for you.
And if you're on a long detour
He'll help you safely through.
He knows where all the speed bumps are
And knows what lies ahead
And He can give you peace and joy
Just like the Bible said.

*I live in a high and holy place, but also with him
that is contrite and lowly in spirit, to revive the
spirit of the lowly Isaiah 57:15*

Heart Song

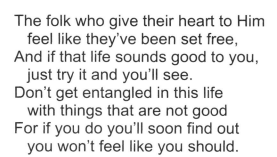

Do you have something
        in your heart
    that makes you want to sing?
There's Someone who's available
    to make the joy bells ring.
A lot of folks have found out how
    and gone straight to the Source,
Make no mistake about it, friend,
    its Jesus Christ, of course.

The folk who give their heart to Him
    feel like they've been set free,
And if that life sounds good to you,
    just try it and you'll see.
Don't get entangled in this life
    with things that are not good
For if you do you'll soon find out
    you won't feel like you should.

So get in touch with Jesus Christ,
    He'll change your heart today
Then you can have a song down deep
    today and every day.

*He put a new song in my mouth,
a hymn of praise to our God.
Psalm 40:3*

Wrinkles

Some faces may show wrinkles
    when years pile up, ya' know,
And they are hard to camouflage
    and fix so they won't show.
But that's not what's important,
    if you keep your spirit sweet
You'll still have friends
        who love you
    and that is hard to beat.

But if your soul gets wrinkled
    and you feel like giving up
Don't wait another minute, friend,
    to let God fill your cup.
He has some stuff for you to do
    for we're His hands and feet--
You might find someone
        needs your help
    who lives just down the street.

God wants your soul in tiptop shape
    to keep you going strong
And He would like to take your hand
    and give your soul a song.
So if you've wrinkles on your face
    just add to them a smile
And keep a twinkle in your eye
    as you walk mile on mile.

I will be glad and rejoice in your love;
Psalms 31:7

All the Same

If you would go to China,
      Taiwan, or Timbuktu,
Or even to Siberia,
      Manila or Peru,
One thing we have in common,
      though we cannot with them talk,
We all smile in the same language
      if we're there and take a walk.
So practice smiling every day
      so you will be in tune
In case you take a trip somewhere
      and go there kinda' soon.
Another reason you should smile
      and sorta' practice up--
It just might brighten someone's day
      and help to fill their cup.

*I will change my expression
and smile Job 9:17*

The Dial
of
Your Heart

When you get up in the morning
And get started on your day
Do you set the dial of your heart
In just a certain way
So you will hear some happy stuff
If whispered in your ear
And if you think on it a bit
You might feel God is near.

Sometimes we keep so busy
That we fail to realize
That God may use a still, small Voice
To whisper from the skies.
So try to calm your pounding heart
Or even take a rest
For when we're kinda' quiet, folks,
We may hear God the best.

Be still and know that I am God;
Psalm 46:10

Just Forgive 'em

If someone is unkind to you
And kinda' gets your goat
You're 'sposed to love your enemies
To keep your life afloat.
If you blast off and say some stuff
That ought not to be said
You may find out you've lost your song
When you crawl into bed.

Sometimes it's hard to handle stuff
That comes across our way
And so we need to think a bit
About the words we say.
The Bible says forgiveness
Is the way to play it smart
And then you won't get ulcers
Plus it will heal your heart.

We also forgive
everyone who
sins against us
Luke 11:4

Doing Your Math

When you wake up in the morning
   do you think to do your math?
Do you count the many blessings
   God has strewn across your path?

If you tell the Lord you're thankful
   for all the stuff you've got
It may help you not to worry
   'bout some things that you have not.

Take time to count your blessings
   when you're starting out your day,
You'll find it makes a difference
   in the things you do and say.

*Were I to count them,
they would outnumber the grains of sand
Psalm 139:18.*

Rocking Chairs

I know some folks can hardly wait
    until they can retire,
They visualize a rocking chair
    before an open fire.
I will admit that sounds right nice
    when days are mean and tough
But sitting in a rocking chair
    sometimes is not enough
To keep a fella' satisfied
    with gladness in his soul
Because his life seems meaningless
    without a worthy goal.
But I've observed some folks I know
    who do that very thing,
They've sorta' lost their grip on life
    and seldom ever sing.
It seems the happiest folks I know
    keep going day by day
And try to help out other folks
    whose skies have turned to gray.
Now as I dwell on this a bit
    I'm sure you'd feel the same--
The happy folks still work and sing
    'til Jesus calls their name.

The Cup-Filler

If you do an act of kindness
And bless some hurting soul
They may remember it for years
And helped to make them whole.
The love you give away, my friend,
Won't die and fade away
But it gets planted in their heart
And grows from day to day.

The folks who spread their love around
And hum and sing and smile
Will find the happiness they want
Is never out of style.
God watches us both day and night
And wants us to look up
Because He's passing good stuff out
And wants to fill our cup.

*for you yourselves have been taught by God
to love each other. 1 Thessalonians 4:9*

Your Cup

When your cup is runnin' over
        you can smile and you can sing
And thank the Lord for all you've got
        with thanks for everything.
God really likes those Thank You prayers
        ascending to the sky
And when I think on it a bit
        I know the reason why.

God gets a lot of messages
        when folks call 911
These frantic calls from folks down here
        keep angels on the run.
So when God hears a loving heart
        not asking for some things
My guess is that He listens hard
        and maybe even sings.

God made us in His Image
        so He has feelings, too,
So talk to Him as your best Friend.
        He'll love it if you do.

Then God said: "Let us make man in our image, in our likeness" Genesis 1:29

*you have filled my
heart with greater joy
Psalm 4:7*

Suspicious Folks?

If you kinda' sing and hum a tune
and smile an awful lot
Folks may become suspicious
and wonder what you've got
That makes your heart so happy
and fills your soul with joy
And things that well could rankle you
does not your peace destroy.

Now if they question you a bit
about your state of mind
Just tell them God lives in your heart
and that they, too, can find
The peace and love that you enjoy
and gives your heart a song
If they will let the Lord on board
and love Him all day long.

Our God does not discriminate
against the black or white
For He is fair and loving
and always does things right.
He'd really like for everyone
to open his heart's door
So He could put a song inside
like they've not had before.

Old Love

We like to go to weddings
 And see the groom and bride
  All gussied up and smiling big
   As they stand side by side,
    Just waitin' for the preacher
     To pronounce them man and wife
      Then rush off on their honeymoon
      And start a brand new life.

We also like to celebrate
 Some older folks, you know,
  Who've lived together time on end
   Like fifty years or so.
    Their love has not eroded
     But has grown throughout the years,
      They've learned to stay on top th' heap
       Through sunshine or through tears.

I think God likes the young folks
 But smiles on oldsters, too,
  I guess God planned it just that way—
   So we'd know what to do.
    It seems we need each other—
     Whether young or old and gray
      And we'll continue to hold hands
       Till God takes us away.

Love never fails. I Corinthians 13:8

Your love has given me great joy and encouragement.

Phileman 7

2

The Joy of Family and Friends

Bedtime Stories

When bedtime stole around each night
    the kids would gather 'round
To hear Dad read a story
    in a children's book he found.
He read of Peter Rabbit,
    or of that scary troll
Whose house was underneath a bridge
    where people took a stroll.

Of course old Humpty Dumpty
    really ended up a mess,
What really happened when he fell
    is anybody's guess.
And Goldilocks went visiting
    the house of three nice bears
And liked a piece of furniture
    when she sat in their chairs.

Sometimes he'd read a story
    from a children's Bible book,
These also were exciting
    for Dad knew just where to look
To find Daniel in the lion's den
    or Jonah in the whale,
Or Jericho's walls all tumbled down—
    their interest did not fail.

Some stuff was kinda' scary
    but that kept their interest up--
When Dad sat down and read to them
    it helped to fill their cup.
They'd go to bed with happy thoughts
    and then drop off to sleep
But first they prayed and asked the Lord
    that He their souls would keep.

Forever Friends

If you have friends you are not poor,
    in fact you're truly blest
For they are much more valuable
    than gold and all the rest.
You can count up all your silver
    and the gold you've slashed away
But it won't love you like a friend
    if you've a rainy day.

I know some folks with lots of dough
    and have a bit of fame
But having cash and having friends
    are really not the same.
A friend will always love you
    whether you are up or down
Or if you live across the tracks
    or on Main Street in town.

So if you have some close, close friends
    be thankful every day
And tell the Lord how blest you are
    when you kneel down and pray.

*there is a friend who sticks closer
than a brother, Proverbs 18:24b*

Special Moments

We all have special moments
That we treasure in our heart,
The time when we got married
And did a family start
And looked upon a newborn babe
Who brought us tons of joy
For children are a special gift,
No matter girl or boy.

It seems God knew a family
Was the best way to go
To bring a lot of love and joy
To folks on earth, ya' know.
It seems these kids are little chips
Straight from the family block
And give us special memories
That in our heart we lock.

I'm glad God made a special plan
To populate the earth
For nothing can exceed the love
Of a new baby's birth.
So if you're blessed with lots of kids
Or only one or two
Thank God you have these special gifts
And that He smiled on you.

Sons are a heritage from the Lord
Children a reward from him. Psalm 127:3

Selective Hearing

It seems to me that kids select
    the things they want to hear;
Its kinda' hard to rise and shine
    till Dad shouts loud and clear:
"The bus is due to be out front
    in ten, or maybe five"--
'Tis when they hear that final call
    that out of bed they dive.

Another time its hard to hear,
    and fills a kid with gloom,
Is when Mom shouts, and points upstairs:
    "You must clean up your room!"
And other words are hard to hear,
    like "take the garbage out,"
Or feed the dog, these, too, can seem
    like foreign words, no doubt.

        I know some kids have hearing loss
            and don't hear very well,
        But they can hear a block away
            the ice cream man's small bell.

Choosing Your Friends

Be careful when you choose your friends
for they'll influence you
In thoughts you think and other stuff
that you will say and do.
Some folks we only know a while
and then they fade away—
They really don't impress us much
as we live day by day.

But there are other folks we meet
that we like quite a lot
Sorta' like a cup of coffee
that really hits the spot.
And so we travel on life's road
and try to play it smart
Aware that lots of folks we meet
leave footprints on our heart.

Walking the Dog?

I know some folks will own a dog
   for it's a friendly pet,
It eats a lot of dog food
   and sometimes sees the Vet.
Of course the Vet advises that
   they should walk their dog
As exercise will help their pet
   to sleep just like a log.

But when I see them walk the dog,
   the dog is in the lead
As if it takes it's master out
   to thank him for its feed.
I wonder if it's possible
   for dogs to realize
It's owner needs
      some good fresh air
   and also exercise.

I 'spose I'll never figure out
   what's in a mongrel's heart,
But I would guess a well-fed dog
   would want to do its part.
So I'll not worry if the dog
   takes its master for a walk
I'll kinda' watch
      from my front door
   while dog and master talk.

Cheer 'em Up

When people come across your path
  I wonder what you do—
I wonder if you cheer them up
  or they leave feeling blue.
Remember, everyone you meet
  could use a bit of cheer
So take the time to say some stuff
  they really need to hear.

And if you cheer 'em up a tad
  it could be you will find
Their attitude might really change
  about the daily grind.
And if they hum and sing a bit
  and make a joyful sound
It really might cause other folks
  to spread their love
    around.

But encourage one another daily
Hebrews 3:18

You Are Special

When I said "Yes" in '45
　　then shortly said "I do"
I didn't know the joy I'd have
　　when I first married you.
　It seems God had a special man
　　dressed in a Navy suit
Who also was a gentleman
　　and really kind, to boot.

Though it was sixty years ago,
　　some things ya' don't forget
I still can see my wedding dress
　　I wore on that day yet.
I didn't have much money
　　so a big ten dollar bill
Was all I paid for it, you know,
　　but still it filled the bill.

We've worked together many years
　　and four kids came along
And we were happy for each one.
　　They filled our lives with song.
We've really done a lot of stuff
　　that most folks do not do
Like going overseas to teach.
　　We also traveled, too.

We went around the world two times
      and saw a lot of things,
   We've been in fifty countries.
         What great joy this travel brings.
      We saw a lot of people
         that we thought were really kind
And meeting different folk abroad
         helped us expand our mind.

How blest we are for sixty years
         that we've walked side by side--
   I didn't know how great you were
         when I became your bride.
      The kindness and the gentleness
         you show from day to day
Says though I'm pretty shaky
         you still love me anyway.

Just Friends

The good Samaritan we know
    was really a nice guy,
He helped a fellow in a ditch
    who was about to die.
The Bible tells that other folks
    who saw the wounded man
Just left him there and passed on by.
    I wonder if they ran.

Some folks are not compassionate,
    they just go on their way
Ignoring folks around them
    who are struggling through the day.
But happy are the loving folks
    who take the time to share
And look out for the hurting ones
    and show them that they care.

It doesn't matter who we are
    or how much stuff we own
We all need love and caring friends
    so we are not alone.

John 4:1 -26

Bitterness

I know that it is not much fun
    to feel depressed and low
When bitterness keeps
        plaguing you
    most everywhere you go.
You want to have a song inside
    and have a happy heart
But you have felt so bad so long
    you don't know where to start.

To harbor bitter feelings
    because someone did you wrong
Can really kinda' get your goat
    and take away your song.
If you would think on it a bit
    I'm sure that you would find
It really is not worth the stress
    to keep it in your mind.

Forgiveness is the only way
    to set your spirit free--
I know it's worked for other folks
    and also worked for me.
Don't let another person
    spoil your life and make you sad,
Forgiving them will heal your heart
    and make your spirit glad.

Get rid of all bitterness Ephesians 4:31

Flawless

If you are looking for a friend
 Who has no flaw nor fault,
  You might as well call off your search
   And bring it to a halt.
    There is no one on planet Earth
     Who's perfect to a "T."
      And if we're honest with ourselves
       Our own faults we might see.
       So if you have a friend or two
       We take folks as they are,
      And they may do the same for us
     Although not up to par.
    This could be why we get along
   With others day by day,
  We've come to know all folks have flaws
 And love them anyway.

*for all have sinned and fall short
of the glory of God   Romans 3:23*

Don't Just Stay At Home

You've been everywhere and you've seen all the sights?
  You've not missed a thing on your multiple flights?
Just slow yourself down to a much slower pace;
  A road map will tell of an interesting place
Like Horse Heaven Hills, Oblong, and Big Foot,
  They might be worth while for a glance or a look.
Then Thief River Falls, also Gully and Hay,
  May be just the place for a wonderful day.
E'en Stinking Creek Road has a sound all its own
  (Before taking that one you may want to phone).
The place that's called Pitts just might be a winner.
  It could be a place for a jolly good dinner.
There's Windfall, and New Hope, and Rattlesnake Hills--
  Now that in itself could produce many thrills.
So get out your map and pack toothbrush and comb.
  You'll miss all these sights if you just stay at home.

Blue Mondays

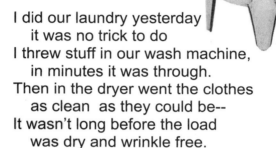

I did our laundry yesterday
   it was no trick to do
I threw stuff in our wash machine,
   in minutes it was through.
Then in the dryer went the clothes
   as clean as they could be--
It wasn't long before the load
   was dry and wrinkle free.

It hasn't always been like this,
   those folks of long ago
Would wash their clothes on Mondays;
   they just would plan it so.
They had a copper boiler filled
   with water from the well,
And on a wood-fired kitchen stove
   they'd wait 'til they could tell

The water would be hot enough
   to melt Fels Naptha soap.
Then they would get the wash tubs out,
   but somehow they could cope.
And in those early, early days
   a washboard was the thing
To scrub the soil out of the clothes,
   most scrubbers didn't sing.

In later years a wash machine
	with wringer came along
And I would guess this new machine
	did help restore their song.
But they were not clear
		through the day,
	the clothes must be hung out,
And hopefully they would be dry
	if days were warm, no doubt.

Then ironing was quite a job--
	on this I will not chat,
And women's lib was quite unknown,
	there was no time for that.
Those country folks were mighty tough,
	they didn't sigh nor shirk,
They did the things they had to do--
	and that was work, work, work.

Some places in the world today
	things still are pretty bad
The ladies head for river banks
	to wash their clothes a tad.
There may be crocodiles around
	or hippos swimming by.
Yet those brave ladies wash their clothes
	and lay 'em out to dry.
So ladies of America,
	remember how you're blest,
How you can run a batch of clothes
	and then lay down and rest.

Take Time

I've thought of young folks of today
    with lots of stuff to do
With cell phones held up to their ear,
    computers nearby, too.
Of course TV and radio
    take time to hear and see--
With all this modern stuff around
    something sorta' bothers me.

    I wonder if kids of today
        hear bedtime stories read
    When all the children gather 'round
        before they're tucked in bed.
    Have they heard of Humpty Dumpty,
        Peter Rabbit, or Bopeep,
    The little girl who tried so hard
        to find her missing sheep.

It seems they're missing something
    if there is no story time
There are lots of things to cheer the heart
    in stories or in rhyme.
So if you have some little folks
    whose love you'd like to keep
Take time to read some stories
    just before they go to sleep.

Just Smile

Don't push the replay button
If someone's done you wrong
For if you do you'll surely find
That you have lost your song.
The folks who even up the score
And ruminate on stuff
May find that hatred is not smart
And makes their life more tough.

Forgiveness heals a lot of wounds
That could one's life destroy
But if we keep a singing heart
It brings us lots of joy.
No matter what one says to you
That kinda' gets your goat
Just look 'em in the eye and smile.
Don't let 'em rock your boat.

*When I smiled at them,
they scarcely believed it;
the light of my face was
precious to them. Job 29:24*

School Days

How fondly I remember
 The little one-room school
  Where I attended as a child
  And learned the Golden Rule.
   My father was a farmer
   And so this was the place
    We went to learn to read and write
And ran hard to first base.

I know the building lacked a lot
 Compared with schools today
  But this small country schoolhouse
  Served the village of Horton Bay.
   And so the kindergarten kids
    Heard stuff up through grade eight
     So they learned things beyond their years
Which in itself is great.

If kids didn't learn the things they should
 When they'd recite in class
  They'd hear it several times again
  So most of them would pass
   And then they'd go to high school,
    Some on to college, too,
     It seemed those country kids were smart
And knew what they should do.

And recess was a special time
 When we went out to play,
  The young kids and the older ones
  Would mingle every day.
   At noon we'd get our dinner pail
   And sit around and eat
     Sometimes we'd find that Mom had packed
Some special little treat.

Don't feel sorry for the children
 Who attend a one-room school--
   They learn a lot and you can bet
They are nobody's fool.

For you make me
glad by your deeds,
O Lord;
I sing for joy at the
works of your hands.

How great are your
works, O Lord

Psalm 92:4,5

3

Loving God's Creation

If We Could . . .

If we could add up all the songs,
Plus gather every book
And then add all the sermons preached
In every church and nook
We couldn't summarize God's love
So folks would understand
How big God is and what He does
And things that He has planned.

And even if we added flow'rs,
And trees of every kind
Plus birds and animals and stars
And other things we'd find
Like mountain peaks and valleys,
And rushing flowing
        streams
No words we have
        can e'er describe
The love of God, it seems.

I guess the best that we can do
Is love God in our heart
And listen when He speaks
        to us
And kinda' get a start
On understanding His great love
And see if we can try
To find the reason He calls us
the Apple of His Eye.

Jesus replied: "Love the
Lord your God with all your
heart" Matthews 22:37

Evening Shadows

When evening shadows are stretched out
There's lots that we can do, no doubt.
It's awfully nice to take a walk
Or sit out on the porch and talk.
With pressures of the day now done
We've time to watch the setting sun;
This is a special time of day
So let it wash your cares away.

Our Awesome Creator

Sometimes I think on things a bit
    that almost blow my mind
And I find God is awesome
    because of what I find.
How could God make big elephants
    and small mosquitoes, too,
And still come up with garter snakes
    and the hopping kangaroo?

Each kind of creature has its mind
    and set of eyes to see;
How God comes up with lots of stuff
    just really baffles me.
It also is amazing how he gave
    the dogs a bark,
It's different from a lion's roar
    and from a meadow lark.

And then the gold and diamonds
    that He tucked inside the earth
Were really nice surprises
    when folks found what they were worth.
God didn't clone a bunch of stuff
    and say that "it's okay
If things aren't really up to par—
    folks won't know anyway."

He never does a half a job
   or leaves his work undone,
He is never on vacation
   just to sit out in the sun.
He knows that folks on planet earth
   need lots of help, ya' know,
And so He always is on call
   if folks are feeling low.

God's really a perfectionist
   and does things up to snuff,
He doesn't get worn out and tired
   and think He's done enough.
And best of all God loves us
   and that's the crowning touch
Of all of His creation
   because He loves us much.

Say to God, "How awesome
are your deeds" Psalm 66:3

Our ID

It really is amazing
 That there is no one like you.
  Your fingerprints and DNA
   Can give the cops a clue
    Of if you're who you claim to be.
     Of if you are a fake
      When someone holds a camera
       And will your picture take.

I know that God knows us so well
 He doesn't need that stuff
  To tell the shape our soul is in
   For He knows well enough
    By thoughts we think and words we say,
     And deeds that we do, too.
      For not a thing escapes His Eye,
       He knows us through and through.

And then I get to wondering
 And muse on it a while,
  Does God have work for everyone
  Who walks earth mile on mile?
   I know that I am only one,
    But do I have a part
     In God's great scheme of things on earth
     To do with all my heart?

It seems we'd please the Lord a lot
 By whispering in His Ear
  And ask how we could serve Him best—
   Those words He'd love to hear.
   God has a place for everyone
    For He needs hands and feet
     To help the folks who need a lift
      No matter town or street.

Birds

I kinda' like to watch the birds—
   when they wake up they sing,
Is it because their needs are met
   and don't need anything?
Do they like their job description
   building nests with bits of grass
And then lay eggs and keep 'em warm
   and wait for time to pass

     Until some baby birds appear,
        then there is work to do
     For little birds have hunger pains
        just like their parents do.
     And so the mom and dad pitch in
        to raise their little brood
     And even teach them how to sing
        and how to find their food.

          It's amazing how the bird brain
             knows how it must survive
          And it is programmed so they know
             how they can stay alive.
          This didn't happen just by chance
             a million years ago
          For God created birds with care—
             He loves their songs, you know.

Penguins

Don't you love the looks of penguins
   as they look all gussied up
Like they have on tuxedos
   to go somewhere to sup?
They're always seen in black and white
   at home or at the beach—
And when they talk among themselves
   I don't understand their speech.

They have scale-like barb-less feathers
   along with flipper wings
But these don't get 'em off the ground,
   but penguins know these things.
It's fun to watch these flightless birds
   go waddling through the snow,
It seems they're in a hurry
   almost anywhere they go.

I'm glad their coat
    of feathers
  keeps them warm
    and looking neat
For they might want
    to chat a while
  with new friends
    that they meet.

Rhinos

Some folks will visit Africa
    and then go on safari
And from the stories that they tell
    they really are not sorry.
Of course it costs a bit of dough
    to take that kind of trip
But if you wait too long
    you just might fall and break a hip.

A lot of things I liked to see,
    but the big black rhino
Was so much bigger than the rest
    you'd think he'd be quite slow.
Although he weighs more than a ton
    don't think he is not fast
Unless you can top 30 miles
    you just might come in last.

His sense of smell is very good,
    his hearing is acute,
But when it comes to seeing things
    it isn't worth a hoot.

Amazingly, this hefty beast
      will charge full speed ahead
And if you're in the critter's way
      you well may end up dead.

I read about a rhino
      that was moved inside a truck
And when the door was open
      he showed he had some pluck
For he took vengeance on that truck
      and rammed it pretty bad
So if you're moving rhinos, friend,
      make sure they are not mad.

The Vet

A doctor who treats animals
    must really be quite smart
For animals can't tell the Doc
    if it's it's head or heart
That makes it feel down in the dumps
    with head a' hangin' low,
And if their tail is dragging,
    they're pretty sick, you know.

The Vet can't understand meows,
    a whinny, or a bark,
I've never heard a ferret talk
    when it hides in the dark.
It must upset the Doc a bit
    when he just has to guess
About the medicine he gives—
    should it be more or less?

When treatment is a guessing game
    for those that cannot speak
And if the Vet says "open wide
    so I can take a peek"
The animal may eye the Vet
    and wonder what he said
And even give a wistful look
    with heart that's full of dread.

I know I could not be a Vet,
    I know I'd sorry be
When cats or dogs or horses
    would look wistfully at me.
I'd prob'ly have to specialize
    on those that can be heard
And only treat the parrots
    and the talking myna bird.

Tree Frogs

Have you ever seen a tree frog
Sitting on your kitchen floor?
It was a little visitor
We'd never seen before.
I'm not too much on wildlife
Sneaking right inside our house
And that includes small lizards
And the hungry little mouse.

Now if I'd want a critter
To share my home and board
I'd have a special place for it
And let it stay aboard.
Now when we took our kitchen broom
To try to shoo it out
We found that little rascal
Was pretty smart no doubt

For when we closed our workroom door
With our computer stuff
It made a jump and found the crack
Was really big enough
And so we have a tree frog
Living in our workroom here
And as long as it keeps quiet
We will not live in fear.

Storms

Last night the wind
      blew really hard,
   it whistled in the dark,
Torrential rain was falling
   on the town of Avon Park.
The people had been watching news
   about a hurricane
And wondered where the thing would land,
   and Wilma was its name.

When morning came I saw the wind
   blow branches back and forth,
Do you suppose their roots hung on
   for all that they were worth?
And birds must have a special touch
   to build a sturdy nest
So they can weather wind and rain
   and really stand the test.

Its kinda' like sometimes in life
   we run into a storm--
It's hard to hunker down again
   where we felt safe and warm.
But be assured the sun will shine
   for God is Lord of all
And if you dial His 911
   He'll hear you when you call.

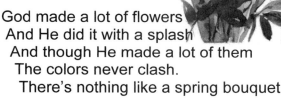

Flowers Are Special

God made a lot of flowers
And He did it with a splash
And though He made a lot of them
The colors never clash.
There's nothing like a spring bouquet
To cheer a weary soul
Especially when loving hands
Arrange them in a bowl.

But not just colors and design
Make flowers hard to beat
God also added perfume
Which I think is pretty neat.
No wonder men take flowers
To their wife or to their date,
Or when they're getting married
And about to cut the cake.

And even when a person leaves
And walks that golden stair
The gift that's most appropriate
We give them then and there.
It seems that flowers say a lot
That words can never say,
That's why God gave His special touch
And made them just that way.

Life's Lemonade

Some folks get bent all out of shape
    when someone does them wrong,
And if they don't forgive it,
    it steals away their song.
First thing ya' know their aches and pains
    will worsen by the day
And its really kinda' stupid
    to live your life that way.

But if your mind says "hold a grudge"
    and keep it in your heart
You're making your life difficult
    which isn't very smart.
We all have bumps and hurts in life
    but we've the power to choose
If they will keep us in the pits
    where we are bound to lose,

Or if we'll throw it in the trash
    and smile and keep our song
And 'fore ya' know it life is good
    and we can travel on.
God wants us to be happy
    and enjoy the things He's made
So if life hands you lemons, friend,
    make a batch of lemonade..

Smarts

I know some folks have lots of smarts
 But cannot figure out
  How birds can migrate miles and miles
  And never seem worn out.
   We know they never have a map
   To show them where to head,
    You'd think their heart and lungs would burst
    And leave the birds half-dead.

I know if we would try to swim
 A thousand miles or so
  Before we'd swim a country mile
  We'd have no get up and go.
   And yet the bird can fly with ease
   To some far distant shore
   And doesn't lose directions
    In a thousand miles or more!

I wonder how the Arctic terns
 Born up near the North Pole
  Leave home when they are six weeks old
  And they are in control
  And fly eleven thousand miles south
   To spend the winter there
   Then they fly back to their old home
   To spend their summer there.

God must have made the bird-brain
Out of special kinds of stuff
Because those birds are awful smart
And must be pretty tough.
There are some folks who ride a plane
And circle planet earth,
Still others take a catamaran
And sail for all they're worth.
And so we find that birds have brains
That tell them what to do,
God also gave smarts to the folks
Who sail the oceans, too.

Trees

I know we've seen a lot of trees
    and oft sit in their shade
But have you counted up the kinds
    of trees that God has made?
The oak, the palm, the evergreen,
    the maple, and the fig,
The sycamore, the beech, the elm,
    tell us that God is big.

I know I've only named a few—
    I sure can't name 'em all,
But have you thought on them a bit,
    how some are big and tall
And have a trunk so thick and broad
    supporting tons of wood?
The roots must hang on awfully tight—
    more than you think they could.

I marvel when the wind blows hard
    and beats against a tree
That it can still stay upright
    and not topple down on me.
The wind and rain and storms that blow
    just tend to make it strong,
God knew how tough they'd need to be
    so didn't do it wrong.

It kinda' makes me think a bit
　　　while we tread earthly sod
There are gonna' be some storms in life
　　　till we get home with God.
No doubt if we can weather them
　　　and keep from giving up
We'll find, like trees, they'll make us strong
　　　and God will fill our cup.

Its Different Now

I know that things have changed a lot
        since I was just a kid--
It seems the folks who grow up now
        don't do the things we did.
We kinda' had our chores at home,
        attended Church and school,
Of course our parents wanted us
        to live the Golden Rule.

When we had extra time for fun
        we might play hide and seek
And that was kinda' fun, ya' know,
        if the seeker didn't peek.
Of course we didn't have a grill
        but if we'd gather wood
We'd light a fire and roast hot dogs
        that tasted mighty good.

I doubt that life at slower speed
        deprived us very much
For we had neighbors who were kind
        and so we kept in touch.
I hope the folks who have a lot
        and rush from place to place
Will take time to enjoy themselves
        and not just take up space.

Stuff

I like the word "stuff" for it covers so much,
   And puts lots of things in a group,
It may be the things we don't know where to put
   Could fit in a file we call "Soup."
There is stuff that we write, and stuff that we mail,
   There's stuff in the closet and car,
There's stuff in our purse, and stuff in the fridge,
   There's stuff wherever we are.
There's stuff that we love and stuff that we hate
   There's stuff we would like to forget,
There's stuff that we want and there's
        stuff that we don't,
   There is stuff we need to do yet.
I know of no word that will cover so much,
   No word that could ever embrace
The odds and the ends of disorganized folk
   When there's stuff all over the place.

*Take heart, daughter,
he said, your faith
has healed you.*

Matthew 9:22

*According to your
faith will it be
done unto you.*

Matthew 9:29

4

According to Your Faith

Figuring It Out

Sometimes we have to scratch our head
  and try to figure out
Why we are here on planet earth
  and what life's all about.
It seems some folks know how to climb
  the ladder of success
While other folks from down below
  just watch 'em climb, I guess.

It seems God gives to us a choice
  to either stand up tall
Or be a couch potato
  and do nothing good at all.
So if you're in that place in life
  just wond'ring what to do
Put your small hand in God's big Hand.
  He has good news for you.

Behind the Scenes

God does some things behind the scenes
   that we don't know about--
Sometimes we wonder, " Why this, Lord?"
   and we begin to doubt
About the things that come our way
   and rankle us a tad
Because it makes no sense to us
   so we start feeling bad.

  But now that I have lived a while
    sometimes I plainly see
  Some things that happened in the past
    were much the best for me.
  God knows what He is doing
    and sometimes it's hard to tell
  The things He's working in our lives
    and does it oh, so well.

So if at times your way seems tough
   and troubles come your way
Remember God's preparing you
   to live with Him
    some day.

*And we know that
in all things God
works for the good of
those who love him
Romans 8:28*

Morning Time

When you wake up in the morning
    and you kinda' scratch your head
    Do you greet the day with gladness
    thanking God you are not dead?
    I think contented folks who smile
    and have a happy heart
    May well prolong their days on earth
if they will do their part.

It's kinda' strange how attitudes
    affect the way we feel,
    They even might affect the way
    that we digest a meal.
    The stomach may appreciate
    a happy heart as well
    So all our parts can smoothly run.
Sometimes it's hard to tell

If stress can do a person in
    so things don't work quite right
    And folks will end up counting sheep
    to get to sleep at night.
    So keep the dial of your heart
    tuned in to happy stuff--
    You may not need those phantom sheep
to live life up to snuff.

God Has A Plan for You

Sometimes when we get kinda' old
   and feeling pretty tired
We feel our work on earth is done;
   we really aren't inspired—
But did you know if you're alive
   God has a plan for you?
Until you walk those streets of gold
   there's stuff that you can do.

      God puts a premium on smiles
         when they reflect God's love,
      The folks who smile a lot will find
         it fits just like a glove.
      There's nothing like the love of God
         to brighten up one's day,
      God doesn't care if you are young
         or if you're old and gray.

So don't get grumpy when you're old
   and don't complain a lot
But try to keep on smiling
   with all the strength you've got.
And be prepared to feel God near
   and hear His loving Voice
For all the folks who live for Him
   will feel their heart rejoice.

Faith

Some people have a lot of faith,
  Some others almost none,
    That could explain why there are folks
    Who have a lot of fun.
      The folks who have their faith in God
      And trust to Him their life
Will find He drains some pressures off
That want to cause us strife.

"According to your faith," my friend,
  "So be it unto you,"
    And that's straight from the Bible
    So we know that it is true.
      To build your faith it helps to read
      Some verses from God's Book
And there are lots and lots of them
  If you'll just take a look.

A favorite is of Jonah
 In the belly of the whale,
  And God was watching while he took
   That under-water sail.
    And Daniel in the lion's den
     Should get your interest up—
At times God uses different ways
To fill a fellow's cup.

The fiery furnace held no fear
 For three young Hebrew men
  For Jesus stood beside them
   So no flames could harm them then.
    How Noah and his family
     Could build that big old ark
Preserving animals and birds
Though it was cold and dark.

Read of David and Goliath,
 And of Paul and Silas, too,
  Remembering they're not fiction
   But all of them are true.
    There is story after story
     Written down to help us cope
That really will amaze you
And increase your faith and hope.

*Then he touched their eyes and said,
"According to your faith will it be
done to you." Matthew 9:29*

Change

A lot of folks who've lived for years
      have seen a lot of change
And most of it is really nice
      but some is kinda' strange.
The horse and buggy days are gone,
      so now we drive a car
To get us where we wanna' go
      though it is near or far.

The clothes we wear don't look the same,
      a lot are wash and wear;
Some folks take medicines galore
      to help with wear and tear.
Of course fast foods are popular
      so folks don't have to cook,
They'd rather watch a movie
      or curl up with a good book.

Computers make folks change a lot,
      now we don't need a stamp
For emails are so fast to write
      we don't get writer's cramp.
Our air conditioned rooms are great,
      our frozen foods are nice,
When we microwave leftover food
      we eat for half the price.

Oh, there are lots of changes
      that will come our way each year
And though sometimes we shift our gears,
      one thing is very clear
We serve a God who changes not,
      His Word's the same today--
We know the Ten Commandments
      are forever here to stay.

So don't be fooled by trifling stuff
      that wants to make you mod,
It's better far to keep your faith
      till you're at Home with God.

Methuselah

I've thought about Methuselah
    who lived so many years,
He must have thought on happy stuff
    and didn't dwell on fears.
Nine hundred sixty nine, ya' know,
    are lots of years to live;
He must have talked to God a lot
    and knew how to forgive.

He may have exercised each day
    and ate good healthy food
For if he ate a lot of junk
    he might have come unglued.
I would doubt that he ate pizza
    and other greasy stuff--
Could he have eaten cornbread
    if times got kinda' tough?

I'm not sure what his diet was
    that made him live so long
But I am sure he loved the Lord
    who gave his heart a song.
Another thing that might have helped
    was there was no TV
For couch potatoes can die off
    if that is all they see.

Back then computers were unknown
  and microwaves were nil,
No planes were flying overhead,
  the atmosphere was still,
I'm sure he lived a different life
  than we folks do today
And must have had great peace of mind
  that made him want to stay.

So if we'd live a long, long time,
  I wonder could it be
We oughta' keep a song inside
  that kinda' sets us free?
If we love God with all our heart
  and serve Him every day
It could be He would let us live
  until we're old and gray.

Genesis 5:21-27

Flower Gardens

When people plant their flowerbeds
     they give them lots of care
And hope the seeds put in the ground
     will come up bright and fair.
They chop the soil and water it
     and even fertilize
Expecting that some blossoms rare
     will soon materialize.

And so these folks will watch and wait
     to see some shoots of green
And when they finally do come up
     its such a lovely scene.
I'm glad the Lord made flowers,
     and He splashed on colors rare
So folks would love to grow 'em,
     and maybe even share.

Another thing amazes me
        is how some plants will grow
And come up through some little cracks
        with not much room ya' know.
It must be God knows how to plant
        and does it with great care
And so if He has planted them,
        they can grow anywhere.

It's kinda' like some people
        who are penniless and poor
And yet they somehow can squeak by
        although they wish for more.
So if you're in a flowerbed
        or growing through a crack
Keep blooming where you're planted
        for the Lord is keeping track.

Always There

Don't wait until disaster strikes
    before you start to pray--
God really likes to keep in touch
    with you each passing day.
He wants to know when times are good
    and also when they're tough
So He can know when you need help
    and give you grace enough.

At times it seems God's far away,
    not knowing where we are,
But be assured He always knows
    if we are near or far.
Some folks will try to hide from God
    but it's a waste of time,
He sees us if we're young or old,
    or if we're in our prime.

Don't hesitate to talk to God,
    don't put your life on "hold"
He wants you to commune with Him
    e'en if the winds blow cold.
It's awfully nice to hunker down
    in His great love and care;
No matter what life hands to us
    our God is always there.

Because He is at my right hand,
I will not be shaken Psalm 16.8

Smile A Lot

Smile a lot, friends, smile a lot—
It makes folks wonder what you've got
That makes you laugh and smile and grin
As if you've something deep within
That's kinda' secret from the rest
And makes you look like you are blest.
You need not have a lot of clout
To show what life is all about.
If you have joy it's gonna' show
So if you have it, let it glow.
A lot of folks could use a smile
And they are never out of style.
So spread your joy and just relax
Then you can live life to the max.

Make 'em Happy

If someone comes across your path
Give them a word of cheer,
It may be they have sought you out
Because of what they'd hear.

Don't spread a word of gossip
But encourage them a tad,
For they may need encouragement
If they are feeling bad.

It's good to make folks happy
And take worry off their chest
Some folks just have a special knack--
It's what they do the best.

Cold Winds

Some days are kinda'
    tough, ya' know,
      when things don't go just right,
It seems no matter what we do
    it seems we feel uptight.
So what's a guy supposed to do
    if he has lost his song?
It may be some would tell us
    that we've done something wrong.

    But if we think on it a tad
      that may not be the case,
    It could be we should talk to God
      about more love and grace.
    There is no easy answer
      when life's winds are blowing cold
    And sometimes they seem stronger
      when we are growing old.

    We really need to hunker down
      in God's great love and care
    And tell Him all our troubles
      and then just leave them there.
    He is good at solving problems
      and loves to hear our voice,
    And if we'll put our hand in His
      He'll make our heart rejoice.

*Come to me all who are weary and burdened
and I will give you rest. Matthew 11:28*

A Day
Brightener

Nehemiah 8:10

When you're tired and discouraged
    do you take the time to look
And see if there's an answer
    in God's most Holy Book?
One verse I really like a lot,
    though not of too much length
Says simply when we have God's joy
    that it will give us strength.

        There are some other nuggets
            I find scattered here and there
        And I delight to read them
            in my kitchen rocking chair.
        "Come unto Me, I'll give you rest"
            renews my spirit, too,
        When I feel pushed and kinda' down,
            with stuff I oughta' do.

Sometimes it comes in handy
    to recall a verse or so
So we can get on top th' heap
    and then get up and go.
At times we do not realize
    there's help not far away
That could give us a joyful sound
    and brighten up our day.

Propping Us Up

Some days when we crawl out of bed
     It's hard to get in gear
And do the stuff we oughta' do,
     although its very clear
That there are things awaiting us
     that really need our touch
And if we really felt quite good
     'twould not amount to much.

But if you don't feel up to par
     and life is kinda tough
There's something you can do, ya' know,
     when you lack strength enough.
Tell God you need His help today
     although you've really tried
And He will help you sure enough
     and prop your leanin' side.

*Look to the Lord and his strength;
seek his face always. Psalm 105:4*

Our Father
in heaven, hallowed
be your name,
your kingdom come,
your will be done
on earth as it
is in heaven.

Matthew 6:9, 10

5

Our Father in Heaven

Asking

I don't ask God for
    too much stuff
for He knows what I need
So I enjoy the things he sends
    and kinda' let Him lead.
I get a lot of joy, ya' know,
    to think that He loves me
And that's as good as it can get
    and sets my spirit free.

I often talk to Jesus
    and will tell Him "Thanks a lot
For all the blessings that I have
    and for the stuff I've got."
God has good things to say to folks
    who take the time to hear,
And when our hearts break forth in praise
    He bends a list'ning ear.

To know your heart is right with God
    and often keep in touch
Gives Him the message loud and clear
    that you love Jesus much.
So when you talk to Him each day
    just try to measure up
And keep your heart's door open wide
    so He can fill your cup.

Fancy Prayers

Some folks use lots of fancy words
    when to the Lord they pray
As if they want to show their skill
    by big words that they say.
I doubt the Lord is too impressed
    by fancy words and such
For if they're only from the head
    they won't amount to much.
I am not sure how God views these,
    to judge is not my part,
But one thing that I know for sure—
    God listens to the heart.

I wonder if you've thought about
        that God is always Home,
You never get beyond His reach
        no matter where you roam.
He's open seven days a week
        and never locks His door
So anyone on planet earth,
        though they are rich or poor

Can talk to Him and tell Him thanks
        for all the stuff they've got
For when they count their blessings up
        they find they have a lot.
And if they have a problem
        they can also share that, too,
And if they tell Him all their heart
        He knows just what to do.

It almost blows my mind, ya' know,
      to think He's always there
And never takes a few days off
      to breathe some country air
And take some time for R and R,
      relaxing just a tad
For it must really weigh Him down
      when things on earth are bad.

The folks who want no part of God
      and do things their own way
Have no one they can turn to
      when they have a lousy day.
So folks thank God He's always Home
      and not locked up at night,
Just put your hand in His big Hand.
      He'll make your burden light.

Quiet Desperation

It seems some folks will spend their life
        in quiet desperation,
They find no joy to cheer their heart
        in all of God's creation.
I know sometimes it's hard to sing
        when skies have turned to gray,
But hard times really come to 'pass,'
        they do not come to stay.

Now if you find you have no song
        and life is mean and tough,
Self-pity will not fill the bill--
        it's really not enough.
You've got to stir yourself a bit
        and count the things you've got;
It's not too smart to make a list
        of things that you have not.

If desperation has set in
        and quietly you groan,
Just put your hand in God's big Hand;
        you'll find you're not alone.

*For I am the Lord your God,
who takes hold of your right
hand. Isaiah 41:13*

Luke 18:9-14

Both Men Prayed

Jesus told a parable one day
 About two different men
  Who both were praying to the Lord
   And 'fore each said, "Amen"
    The one told God how great he was
    And good things that he did,
     No doubt he went to church a lot
     Since he was just a kid.

     He said he always paid his tithe
      And fasted twice a week,
       He liked to pray so folks could hear
       The bragging words he'd speak.
        This Pharisee talked on and on
        And said a lot of stuff
        And then told God the other man's
       Not living up to snuff.

      The other man, a publican,
       Did not have much to say
        But smote his breast and bowed his head
       And God heard him that day
       For he said, "I'm a sinner, Lord,
      Be merciful to me,"
     And this man went home justified
    And happy as can be.

I Love Your Word, Oh Lord

I love to read Your Word, Oh Lord,
    it means a lot to me,
For there's wisdom in its pages
    that can set a person free.
It tells us how we ought to live
    for living at its best
And if we do the things it says
    we'll have both peace and rest.

It tells us of the patriarchs
    who lived in days of old
And though we've heard of them as kids
    they still are often told
Like Daniel in the lion's den,
    and David and his sling,
Of course when Samson's hair was cut
    it spoiled most everything.

There's Moses and the burning bush,
    and Jonah and the whale,
And these and many more are told
    of God who did not fail.
And then in the New Testament
    some lived when times were bad
Some Christians got some beatings
    taking all the grace they had.

But there were also happy times
      when Jesus healed the blind
And even brought folks back to life,
      for He was super kind.
He gave the Sermon on the Mount
      and taught us how to pray,
The things He taught aren't out of date
      but still are used today.

Besides the heroes in God's Book,
      it gives in great detail
How Christians can prepare for Heav'n
      and make it without fail.
So when you knock on Heaven's Gate
      and walk that golden stair
Please be assured inside your heart
      King Jesus will be there.

The Sacrifice of Praise

Since Jesus Christ was Crucified
　　　and shed His Blood for man
He was the all-time Sacrifice
　　　according to God's Plan.
We no more offer bulls and goats
　　　to take away our sin
For God devised a different way
　　　to give us life within.

God still wants us to sacrifice
　　　in several kinds of ways--
I kinda' like to give to God
　　　the Sacrifice of Praise.
It makes me happy when I thank
　　　the Lord for what I've got
For He has blessed me bountifully
　　　and given me a lot.

I feel the Lord is really pleased
　　　when we've good stuff to say,
I think the Sacrifice of Praise
　　　might really make His day.

*Let us continually offer to God
a sacrifice of praise. Hebrews 13:15*

Trying Out Stuff

Some folks will try a lot of stuff
        to try to help them cope
So they can stay on top th' heap
        and give them joy and hope.
Some may buy fancy cars and clothes
        and eat expensive meals
And if their health in kinda' poor
        they may get Meals on Wheels.

The Bible has good news for those
        who struggle for life's best
It says if we will come to God
        He'll give us peace and rest.
Some folks have learned this secret
        and they look to God each day
For guidance and protection
        and for help along life's way.

Small Prayers

When children say their prayers at night
before they fall asleep
Their trusting little hearts will ask
the Lord their soul to keep.
They also ask that if they die
before they should awake
They want God to remember them
so He their soul will take.

I'm sure God's heard that childish prayer
repeated o'er and o'er
No doubt it's in the millions—
even billions, maybe more.
But Jesus loved the little kids--
I'm sure He takes time out
To listen to a little child
and things they talk about.

I Prayed for You

Today I prayed for you, my friend,
  I just want you to know
  That you are thought about and loved
  More than you'll ever know.
  I realize that living
  Can sometimes steal your song
  But God has ways to cheer the heart
When minor things go wrong.

Don't forget God watches sparrows
  So you know He watches you
  So keep it in your heart and mind
  He knows all things you do.
  You are the apple of His Eye—
  He wants for you the best
  And if you keep your hand in His
He'll give you peace and rest.

God never is surprised, ya' know,
  At things that come your way
  And be assured He'll give to you
  The strength you need each day.
  So keep a song deep in your heart,
  And if you will look up
  He will come by in His great love
And fill your empty cup.

Keepin' In Touch

God's really awfully good to us
    to tell us not a thing
About just what the future holds
    and what each day will bring.
He knows that we might get upset
    and be depressed and blue
And so He hides the future
    so we won't give up and stew.

      It could be that He much prefers
          to give us strength each day
      For any problems that come up
          to muddy up our way.
      I think God likes it best this way
          so He can keep close touch
      And also let us know for sure
          He loves us very much.

God is Always Listening

I bet the Lord bows down His ear
    and likes it quite a lot
When people pray and give Him thanks
    for all the stuff they've got.
He really knows our every need
    so He takes care of things
So why not just say, "Thank You, Lord"
    and find the joy it brings.

Of course our God would like for us
    to often keep in touch,
He'd like to hear you tell Him
    that you love Him very much.
And while you're on the line with Him
    you oughta' ask Him, too,
If He has something in His Heart
    He'd like for you to do.

Don't live a mediocre life
    and kinda' drift along--
God has a special plan for you
    to give your heart a song.
Don't miss the joy of serving God
    for it's so good to know
That He will keep His Eye on you
    and never let you go.

"on call"

Some folks don't seem to realize
   God always is "on call"
And it's unfortunate to see
   their God is far too small.
When they don't have their head on straight
   they follow rabbit trails
And may end up lost in the woods
   because their judgment fails.

Our God is really wise, ya' know,
   and if folks want life's best
They need to talk to Him a lot
   and let Him be their Guest.
He's always been in Heaven
   and He runs the Place with care
And folks who give their heart to Him
   will live with Him up There.

Don't trust your life to lesser things
   when there's so much at stake
For if your heart is filled with joy
   it will a difference make.
A person who will talk to God
   and on Him often call
Discovers living at its best
   for their God isn't small.

Long Prayers

Some folks say long and fancy prayers
That don't get off the ground.
I'd guess those prayers are not sincere
And have a hollow sound.
It's not too good to just say words
If they're not from the heart--
God knows if they're sincere or not
Right from the very start.
So if you'd speak with God, My friend,
And catch His listening ear
You've gotta' tell it like it is
If you want Him to hear.

The
Listener

It really kinda' blows my mind
About this thing called prayer,
Nobody can prevent it
For our God is always There.
We can pray for someone far away
Or someone right next door
For distance doesn't bother God,
He always knows the score.

God hears the prayers of little folks,
Or those who say a prayer
Because they feel depressed and down
And need someone to care.
But if you think on it a bit
We need God every day
To help us with the bumps in life
That seem to come our way.

Don't hesitate to pray for folks
Who mean a lot to you
For they have struggles all their own--
Needing love and caring, too.
No one can stop a person's prayers
No matter how they try
For God is always listening
Somewhere up in the sky.

Refinement

When your life is going smoothly
    and you're perking right along
It's easy to be cheerful
    if you haven't lost your song.
But if you get too busy
    and you don't take time to pray
You just may hit a speed bump
    that will slow you on your way.

And when these tough times slow you down
    no doubt you'll breathe a prayer
And tell God what your problems are
    assuming He's up There.
Sometimes it's easy to forget
    the good stuff that you've got
Until it sorta' slips away
    and then you're on the spot.

But if you're kinda' in that shape
    and hardly can endure
Remember God still loves you,
    of this you can be sure.
It could be He's refining you
    so He can shine through you
So folks can see the love of God
    in everything you do.

Lord when did we see you hungry and feed you, or thirsty and give you something to drink?
The King will reply "I tell you the truth whatever you did for the least of these brothers of mine, you did for me

Matthew 25:37, 40

6

Being God's Hands and Feet

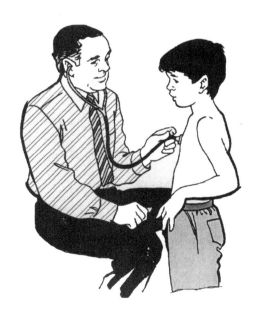

Dressing Up

Some folks will get all gussied up
   and wonder where to go
Because they want to show stuff off
   and strut about, ya' know.
I wonder if they realize
   folks really aren't impressed
By all the trappings and their gold
   and if they look well dressed.

I think a lot of folks I know
   like folks who love and care
About the needs of other folks
   so help 'em out and share.
It's nice to have some fancy stuff
   to wear and to enjoy
But happy are the loving folks
   who bring to others joy.

Leaving Footprints

It's kinda' hard to hold our tongue
 And not judge other folks--
  When they don't do the things we do,
   We think they are a hoax.
    We like to think that we are right
     In things we do and say
      And though we don't agree with them,
       We love them anyway.

    If we are living like we should
     Folks might want what we've got.
      And if we tell 'em what we have
       'Twould please the Lord a lot.
      Sometimes we might be careless
     And think "no one watches me,"
    But let me tell you, friend of mine,
You're wrong as you can be.

If Jesus' love shines through you
And comes from inside out
You'll leave your footprints on their heart,
I've not the slightest doubt.

Helping Others

If you show kindness to someone
      I'm sure that you will find
Not only are they happy
      but you'll have peace of mind.
It's kinda' strange it works that way
      but sure enough it will
For while you're helping other folks
      the Lord your cup will fill.

To help some folks by doing stuff
      is never out of style
And if you want to do it right
      you'll do it with a smile.
If someone is a problem
      that you work with day by day
It could be if you'd smile at them
      some good might come your way.

Some folks are quite a challenge
        to love them in your heart
But why not tackle lonely folks
        and kinda' do your part
To make them feel important
        and you'd like to be their friend—
It could be that some TLC
        a hurting heart could mend.

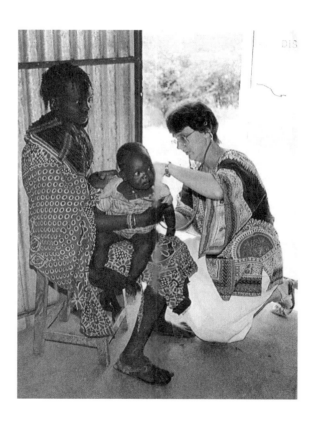

Living in Style

Some people are so busy
 Climbing ladders to success
 They miss a lot of joys in life
 And so end up a mess.
  Instead of watching sunsets,
   Making friends, and smelling flowers
  They're bent on being "big shots"
   Throughout the daylight hours.

  I'm not too sure that lots of dough
  Brings happiness of heart
  Unless they help some hurting folks
 And kinda' do their part.
  So take time for all the good stuff
 God made for us to see
And folk who take the time to look
Are happy as can be.

And so if God has blessed you
 Try to spread His love around
  For lots of folks would like to hear
 A happy, joyful sound.
  Life is kinda' what we make it,
   We can growl or we can smile.
    Forget about those ladders, folks,
    And live your life in style.

Brighten Someone's Day

If you talk about your problems
    when you're chatting with your friends,
They may be looking for the time
    your conversation ends.
They've troubles of their own, you know,
    and sometimes life is tough,
And if they're working hard to cope
    they've problems quite enough.
So don't unload on those you love,
    they'll hate to see you come
If all the things you say to them
    will leave them down and glum.
It's better far to tell your friends
    how blest you are today,
And greet them with a smile and hug
    and brighten up their day.

Shining for Jesus

Let the love of Christ shine through you
As you live from day to day
For lots of folks need cheering up
To drive the blues away.

Some travel on a lonely road,
At times that trail is rough
And they could use a smile or hug
So they'll have strength enough
To make it through life's winding road
And maybe even smile
For if they have a song inside
It makes the trip worthwhile.

The same is true for everyone
Who treads this earthly sod--
We all need some encouragement
Till we're at home with God.

Getting A Song

When you read the morning paper
　does it fill your heart with cheer
Or do you kinda' wince a bit
　at things you read and hear?
I know we need to know some stuff
　that's going on today
But could the news folks add good things
　that happen every day?

Not everything is bad ya' know,
　some good things happen, too,
And how we'd like to hear some stuff
　that's happy and is true.
It would be nice to hear about
　some folks who volunteer
And do nice things for hurting folks
　that bring them joy and cheer.

Some folks would like a phone call
　or a knock upon their door
That lets them know that they are loved
　e'en if they're sick and poor.
God smiles on folks who show their love
　by things they say and do
And He's aware of everything
　so gives a song to you!

Happiness

When we went to Church this morning
      I heard the pastor say
That if you own a lot of stuff
      it's really quite okay
But it won't make you happy
      and give you peace of mind
'Cause you can't take it with you
      up to Heaven you will find.

You're better off to love the Lord
      and give Him all your heart--
To love your neighbor as yourself
      is really pretty smart.
Sometimes we need to think a bit
      about how blest we are
And share the good stuff that we have
      with folks not up to par.

I've lived on earth a long, long time
      and I can plainly see
That people who are givers
      seem as happy as can be.
I've seen some folks with lots of dough
      that buy and buy and buy
But they cannot buy happiness
      no matter how they try.

God gives to us so we can give
        and spread God's love around
For lots of folks sure need to hear
        a happy, joyful sound.
And if you give someone some joy
        and kinda' lift 'em up
You'll find that God will bless you
        and even fill your cup.

remembering the words the Lord Jesus
himself said: "It is more blessed to give
than to receive." Acts 20:35

Hands

God made us in His image
  so He gave us hands, ya' know.
For if we didn't have them
  we'd have no get up and go.
We couldn't write a letter
  and we couldn't sign a check
Nor could we play our table games
  and shuffle up the deck.

We couldn't even tie our shoes
  or cook a tasty meal
For if a person had no hands
  how could he onions peel?
How would one clean the kitchen floor
  and tidy up the house
Or even put a bit of cheese
  to trap a wayward mouse?

We couldn't use computers
  nor could we pick a flower
Life would truly be a hassle
  every day and every hour.
We couldn't hold our children's hands
  when walking in a park
And give their hand a little squeeze
  when it is getting dark.

Sometimes we do not realize
  how blest we really are
That God gave us a pair of hands
  and made us up to par.
We know His Hands stay busy
  looking after folks down here
And He sets the example
  that we oughta' spread some cheer.

So take a look at your own hands
  and thank the Lord today
That He has made you like you are
  and fold your hands and pray.
And when you get up off your knees
  you may soon want to start
To use the hands He's given you
  by blessing someone's heart.

*Whatever your hands find to do,
do it with all of your might.
Ecclesiastes 9:10*

Opportunities

Most of us are common folk,
    we haven't come to fame,
And there are some who've blown the chance
    to get a famous name.
But if, my friend, this sort of thing
    has come to pass for you,
You need not throw the towel in—
    there's stuff that you can do.

God knows what you are doing
    and watches you a lot
So help some folks around you
    and give it all you've got.
If you are working for the Lord,
    my friend, do it with class
For He keeps track of things you do,
    He doesn't let it pass.

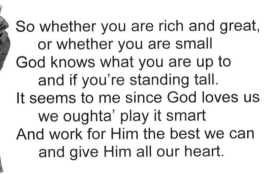

So whether you are rich and great,
    or whether you are small
God knows what you are up to
    and if you're standing tall.
It seems to me since God loves us
    we oughta' play it smart
And work for Him the best we can
    and give Him all our heart.

Comin' in First

It's kinda' strange how some folk feel
    that they are number one
And that they're more important
    because of what they've done.
If they would think on this a bit
    they just might come in last
Because they glorify themselves
    and live their life too fast.

The Good Book says both loud and clear
    that common folks may find
That they may come in first, ya' know,
    and have great peace of mind
Because they help the hurting folks
    and lend a listening ear
And take the time to spread around
    some love, and hope, and cheer.

It's when we are Christ's hands
    and feet
  and do the things He'd do
That gives folks some encouragement
    if they are feeling blue.
Don't envy other folks you know,
    but humbly do your part,
It well may be you'll come in first
    and God will bless your heart.

The Givers

Not many folks have servant's hearts,
   folks find so much to do,
And so we find that helping folks
   is done by just a few.
But those who go as volunteers
   and cheer folks up a tad
Arrive home feeling mighty fine
   and in their heart they're glad
They took the time to help someone
   and went the second mile
For if one gives part of ones-self
   how can he help but smile?

Not many folks with selfish hearts
   will hum and sing a song--
And if they think they're number one
   their focus is all wrong.
We find that joy and peace and love
   the servant's heart will bless
For folks who spread their love around
   find they have happiness.

Not many folks have servant's hearts
     for it takes time, you know,
To spend some time and energy
     with folks whose steps are slow.
It seems the world keeps rushing on
     and some folks cannot find
The happiness they're looking for
     and quiet peace of mind.

No matter if they shop and shop
     and have more than enough
They can't fill up an empty heart
     with selfish kinds of stuff.
The Bible says that happy folks
     will love and serve a lot
So why not go the second mile
     and give it all you've got?

Your Greatest Gift

The greatest gift that
   you can give
to God or anyone
Is giving of yourself, ya' know.
   It's really number one.
Some folks will write a check to help
   or maybe send a card,
And both are really, really nice
   if someone's way is hard.

But if you give them of yourself
   and chat with them a while
It lets them know that they are loved
   and may bring them a smile.
There're lots of ways to show your love
   so folks know that you care
It might be just a simple thing
   like combing someone's hair.

It may be you could baby sit
   so Mom could get some rest
Or if the laundry bag is full,
   to wash it may be best.
I'd guess God blesses servant folks
   who work for Him and smile
And if you're working for the Lord
   do it, my friend, with style.

What God Likes

If you find jealousy and pride
Tucked deep down in your heart
It's best if you get rid of it
And really play it smart.
Your heart can only hold so much
So let it overflow
With love and kindness, peace and joy,
Wherever you may go.

A lot of folks are hurting
And they need a joyful sound
And that's why it's important
To spread your love around.
The world does not need bitterness
And other worthless stuff
So brighten up your corner
And keep it up to snuff.

If you will smile and sing and hum
You'll find your life is blest
Because a heart that's full of love
Is what God likes the best.

Smiles Help

Don't knock a fella' down, my friend,
by unkind words you say,
You won't feel good about yourself
to spoil another's day.
Instead just look folks in the eye
and give a great big smile,
It could be it might make their day
and bless them for a while.

A lot of folk need cheering up
for sometimes life is tough,
They even get depressed and down
when life's not up to snuff.
So give folks smiles instead of frowns
and try to cheer them up
And you will find when you do this
the Lord will fill your cup.

Face To Face

As you look into the mirror
When you've just crawled out of bed
What is the face that greets you,
Does it smile or look half-dead?
Some folks will get up cranky
And it takes a little while
For them to get all gussied up
And then put on a smile.

But what's behind that face of yours,
Does it show strain and stress?
The face you wear quite simply shows
What's in your heart, I guess.
So keep your heart tuned up and full
Of love and joy and grace
So when you get your mirror out
You'll see a happy face.

Staying On Top th' Heap

Do you have much to sing about
　　or is life pretty drab
And all you have to think about
　　are things that once you had?
Your heart can get quite empty
　　if you fail to prime your pump,
For if your attitude is bad
　　you'll fall into a slump.

　　Sometimes we get quite out of breath
　　　　to stay on top th' heap,
　　So its important that we know
　　　　that God our soul will keep.
　　So when you're feeling kinda' blue
　　　　and life has let you down
　　Look up, and count your blessings,
　　　　wear a smile and not a frown.

God cares for people everywhere,
　　no thing is new to Him,
So give your troubles all to God
　　when life is bleak and dim.

*Cast all your cares on
the Lord and he will
sustain you; Psalm 55:22*

Living to the Max

Be careful what you think about,
 It could affect your health;
  And if you live down in the pits
   It could affect your wealth.
    The Bible says a happy heart
     Is like a medicine
      And so our health may quite depend
      By what we find within.

If we are angry and upset
It gets us off the track,
It isn't worth the hassle
To let our lives get out o' whack.
Then we do stuff we shouldn't do,
And say an unkind word
And folks are disappointed
By the things they've seen and heard.

    So think good thoughts,
     And even try to whistle now and then,
      If you encourage other folks
     They may wonder where you've been.
    To think on happy things, my friend,
   Is what you oughta' do
  So you can live life to the max
And be a blessing, too.

If anyone hears my voice and opens the door, I will come in and eat with him and he with me.

Revelation 3:20

7

If Anyone Opens The Door

Only God

No one but God could make a plan
  like for our Savior's birth
And have it orchestrated right
  when He came down to earth.
The governor imposed a tax
  that everyone must pay
So people were all hurrying
  to get well on their way.

And Joseph led a donkey,
  a lowly beast, you know,
To an Inn where they could spend the night
  and then get up and go.
And Mary, who was great with child,
  was anxious to lie down
And kinda' get a breather
  in that sleepy little town.

To think the Inn was full that night
  and with no place to go
They were allowed to spend the night
  in a stable down below.
Of course you know the story well
  that Christ was born that day
And Joseph filled a manger
  with some nearby straw and hay.

*. . . and she gave birth to her first born,
a son. She wrapped him in clothes and
placed him in a manger because there was no
room for them in the Inn. Luke 2:6,7*

No one who stayed inside the Inn
     had offered them their room,
It seems they were too busy
     with their own stuff, I presume.
I really like that shepherds
     were the first to make it there
Because a choir of angels sang
     and told them when and where

They'd find the place where Jesus Christ,
     the Son of God, was born,
And sure enough they found the place
     on that first Christmas morn.
God didn't send his Son, you know,
     to folks who reeked with fame,
He sent Him to the common folks
     who'd be so glad He came.

So if you're rich or if you're poor,
     and have an empty cup
Just give your heart to Jesus Christ.
     He'd love to fill it up.

Zacchaeus

Sometimes I think of Zacchaeus
who climbed up in a tree
For he was just a little man
and Christ he could not see
Because the crowd of bigger folks
were walking in his way
And that is just exactly why
he climbed a tree that day.

I think its neat he ran ahead
and climbed a sycamore,
Apparently he'd never seen
how Jesus looked before.

Zacchaeus was a wealthy man
and was not liked a lot
For he collected taxes
cheating folks right on the spot.
It could be that he took off work
on this one special day
And had determined in his heart
he'd see the Lord some way.

And in my mind's eye I can see
him run that dusty trail
Then shimmy up the sycamore—
he'd see Christ without fail.

And sure enough when Jesus came
   he called him by his name
And after he had met the Lord
   he never was the same.

He said that he would give the poor
   a half of all his stuff
And also added something more,
   as if that weren't enough--
He said if he had cheated folks
   he'd pay 'em back fourfold
But that is not the end of it
   for after that we're told
That Jesus would have lunch with him,
   He'd be his honored guest
And so this little man was changed
   to one whose heart was blest.

Luke 19:1-10

Mary

If you've ever had a baby
    you no doubt had gone by car
And checked in at a hospital
    which wasn't very far.

The doctor and the nurse in charge
    did the admission stuff
And put you in a nice clean bed
    and gave you meds enough
To help you through the labor pains
    until your child was born
And then you got to see your babe,
    though you were tired and worn.

I wonder if you've thought about
    how Mary, great with child
Could travel many weary miles
    and still be meek and mild
When they would come up to the Inn
    where she could get some rest
And find the place was all filled up,
    though Joseph did his best.

I wonder just what Mary thought—
do you think that she sighed
When she lay on a bed of straw, and
maybe even cried?
I doubt she had much stuff along to
make a cozy place—
She must have prayed to God a lot
to give her strength and grace.
Who ever thought this humble place
would welcome such a Guest
Who truly is the King of kings, the
Best of all the best.

Luke 2:4-7

Come, Follow Me
Matthew 4:18-20

I often think how Jesus called
 His disciples here on earth,
  He didn't question them and ask
  Just how much they were worth,
   Nor did he hand out questionaires
   With pages to fill out
    And ask for several references
    To check them out, no doubt.
     He didn't discuss benefits;
      There was no dotted line
       Where if they measured up OK
      A contract they would sign.
     He didn't ask about their past
     Nor for a resume
      He simply said, "Come, follow Me,"
     And it 's like that today.
     Christ is still saying,"Follow Me,"
    And if we hear His voice
  And follow Him where e'er He leads
He'll make our hearts rejoice.

Christ Loved Kids

I wonder if you've thought about
    why Christ loved children so.
Was it because their little hearts
    have lots of love, you know?
They don't have stuff like sin and hate
    stored up inside their heart
So they can kinda' be themselves
    which really is quite smart.

Some older folks with lots of clout
    may put on lots of airs,
But Jesus cuts right through that stuff
    because He really cares.
Christ tells us in the Bible
    that we should all become
Like children with their simple trust
    and love for every one.

I'm sure the Lord likes simple faith
    that has no fear or doubt
For He likes folks who trust in Him
    right from the inside out.
So copy little children
    in the love they shed abroad
For Jesus says to live that way
    till we're at home with God.

Just As We Are

If you are out of work, my friend,
And need a job to do,
You may look several places
That you think appeal to you.

Of course they'll want a resume
Of where you worked before,
They'll also want an interview
When you walk through their door.

You've got to look quite classy
Just to meet the standards there,
And so you gussy up a bit,
Might even curl your hair.

So if you can impress the folks
Who work in personnel
It may be you will land a job
Because you look so well.

But that is not the way with God,
He takes us as we are,
We don't fill out a questionnaire
Though we're not up to par.

St. Peter will not ask us
For a lengthy interview,
God simply wants a humble heart
That He can make anew.

He takes the sick, the blind, the lame,
And those who cannot cope,
No matter if they're rich or poor
He offers them some hope.

He never leaves us as we are
If we give Him our heart,
He changes us from what we were
Right from the very start.

Still Speaking

God is still speaking, friend of mine,
        He hasn't left us here
To travel on life's road alone—
        in fact He's always near.
But if you want to hear Him
        and see things that He has done
You've gotta' get your heart in tune
        and not stay on the run.

God speaks to us through sunsets,
        and through a gentle breeze,
He also speaks through flowers,
        the singing birds, and trees.
The Bible says He's everywhere
        so if you'd look a bit
You really might find it is true
        if you'll just think on it.

Sometimes God speaks in special ways
        that tells us of His power
When thunder rolls and lightning comes
        and skies pour down a shower.
At other times we feel God speak
        in quiet gentle ways
And somehow comes and fills our cup
        with music and with praise.

Some folks will say there is no God
        or that He's far away
And so they took off their list
        and seldom ever pray.
But happy are the many folks
        who feel God is their Friend
And hold to His unchanging Hand
        until the very end.

My Kitchen Window

I like my kitchen windows
        where I can see outside.
It's fun to watch the neighbors
        when they go out for a ride.
Or maybe some will take a walk
        escorted by their dog
And some are really in good shape
        and find it fun to jog.

At times I see some other things—
        some birds go flying by
I guess they want some stuff to eat
        and so they really try.
Some butterflies might make the scene
        and add a touch of class,
A friendly neighbor might drop in.
        I'm glad they didn't pass.

The clouds intrigue me quite a bit—
        the white against the blue
And sunsets add great color
        and we enjoy that, too.
It blows my mind to wonder how
        God made the things He made
Including lots of flowers and trees
        for beauty and for shade.

Another thing I like to watch
        are lizards on the screen
They travel 90 miles an hour
        if you know what I mean.

Our God created everything
     that's found on planet earth
He didn't make some junky stuff,
     but made all things of worth.

Yes, I like my kitchen windows
     so I can see outdoors--
It's much more interesting to me
     than news of floods and wars.
So if you'd spend some worthwhile time
     pull up your kitchen chair
And enjoy all the beauty
     that is waiting for you there.

The Greatest Jesus

Whoever thought that
    Jesus Christ
    born in a stable dim
Would spend His life
    in healing folks
    if they believed in Him?
The common people loved Him much
    and liked the words He spoke,
He spent a lot of time with them
    though some were sick and broke.

Whoever thought this Son of God
    who changed folks life so much
Would some day be hung on a cross
    by some who felt His touch.
But even greater, who would think
    that this unusual Man
Would change the world forever
    as no other person can?

And now each time we write the date
    it points to Jesus' birth,
For He's the greatest Person
    who has lived on planet earth.

Today in the City of David a Savior
has been born to you, He is Christ the Lord
Luke 2:11

Unconditional Love

God's love is unconditional,
    His heart is open wide
To any who'll believe in Him
    and want His love inside.
His eyes are searching everywhere
    on planet earth, you know,
For folks who want to serve Him here
    and then to Heaven go.

There is no case too hard for Him,
    no heart He cannot touch
If folks will give their heart to Him
    and really love Him much.
God's love is unconditional,
    but we must do our part
And tell Him we invite Him in
    to live within our heart.

Just: "Follow Me"

When Christ called His disciples
    He didn't tell them then
That he was making up a group
    of very special men.
He didn't ask where they were born
    or of their family tree,
He only said just two short words,
    and that was "Follow Me."

He could have questioned every man
    and learned a lot of stuff
But all He said were those two words
    And that seemed to be enough.
We can complicate religion
    with all our don'ts and do's
And kinda' fail to follow Christ
    because of things we choose.

If we love God with all our heart,
    our body, soul and mind
It truly is to follow Christ
    and gives us peace of mind.
I really like the way that Christ
    said simply "Follow Me"
And folks who do that very thing
    are happy and set free.

As he walked along, he saw
Levi son of Alphaeus sitting at
the tax collectors booth. "Follow
me" Jesus told him. And Levi
got up and followed him.
    Mark 2:14

In my Father's house are many rooms; if it were not so, would have told you. I am going there to prepare a place for you. . I will come back and take you to be with me that you also may be where I am.

John 14:2,3

8

I Go to Prepare a Place for You

Finally Home

Have you noticed in the book of Psalms
 A very special verse
  That gives the Christian lots of hope
   Although it's kinda' terse?
    It says that when folks die on earth
     It's precious in God's sight,
      We might have known if God's involved
He'd really do it right.

We know that when our kids come home
 To spend a week or so
  We get our house prepared for them
   With things they like, you know.
    We welcome them with open arms
     And try to do our best
      So they'll know they are loved a lot
And are our special guest.

On earth it's difficult to give
 A tearful last goodbye
  But if we think on it a bit
   We maybe shouldn't sigh
    Because God has a place prepared,
     The Welcome sign is clear
      And He keeps waiting for the time
His children will appear.

So while we struggle here on earth
 To let a loved one go
  The ones who are in Heaven
   Are rejoicing for they know
    Another child has made it Home
     And they will always stay
      Where there is happiness and love
Forever and a day.

*Precious in the sight of the Lord
is the death of His saints.
Psalm 116;15*

God Loves Color

We see a lot of pretty stuff like
 flowers, birds, and trees,
And if a person takes a walk
 he lots of beauty sees.
It must be God loves color
 for He used it everywhere;
It could be He had extra paint,
 and so with some to spare
He even painted lots of shells
 all hidden in the sea
And made them very beautiful,
 I know you will agree.

But shells are not the only things
 all hidden from our view
For way down deep inside the earth
 are lots of jewels, too.
The rubies and the diamonds
 do not grow on trees, you know,
And gold and other precious things
 are hidden down below.

When I see earth so beautiful
    for our enjoyment here
It makes me wonder what's in Heaven
    and how it will appear.
We know it must be beautiful
    and we cannot compare
The things that we have seen down here
    with what will be up there.

Some folk believe they've lots of smarts
    and know a lot of stuff
But when it comes to Heaven, folks,
    our minds aren't big enough
To visualize the things we'll see
    and how it looks up there
When we are finished with this life
    and walk that Golden Stair.

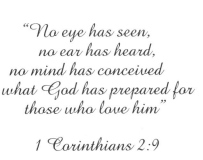

"No eye has seen,
no ear has heard,
no mind has conceived
what God has prepared for
those who love him"

1 Corinthians 2:9

But When We Get to Heaven . . .

When oldsters gather in a group
    and kinda' chew the fat
They'll sit and spin their yarns, ya' know,
    that covers this and that.
But one thing seems to head the list—
    they're going to see the Doc
So he can tune 'em up a bit
    and kinda' wind their clock.

The weather is another thing
    they'll find to talk about
For if a storm is on its way
    they'll have more aches, no doubt.
The price of gas may be discussed,
    they think its much too high,
Their pensions are not adequate
    for things they'd like to buy.

They'll talk about their grandkids
      and just how smart they are,
And even say some church folks
      are not living up to par.
A lot of stuff will be discussed
      by members of the group
But they'll keep chatting on and on
      while eating chicken soup.

But when we get to Heaven, folks,
      this stuff will be forgot
And we'll not talk of aches and pains
      and stuff that we have not.
No one will be complaining on that
      happy golden Shore
Where all things will be perfect and
      we'll live forevermore.

Heaven

I've never been to Heaven
But I hope to go some day
And when I reach that lovely Place
I'm sure I'll want to stay.
After living for a lot of years
Down here with toil and fear
It sure will be lots different
When all problems disappear.

We'll never have to phone in sick
Or have a tire go flat,
Or get a tune-up from the Doc,
Or walk the dog or cat.
We'll not get hit by hurricanes,
Tsunamis won't be There,
No families will be arguing,
There'll be no pain or care.

No one will be complaining
About how bad they feel
And how it almost wears 'em out
To just prepare a meal.
Your neighbors or your boss at work
Won't make you lose your smile
And if you find you need a nap
There'll be time to rest a while.

God is the CEO, you know,
And keeps things up to snuff,
He has a limitless supply
Of lots and lots of stuff.
It's hard for me to figure out
Why all folks don't prepare
And live for God down here on earth
So they can live up There.

They will be his people, and God himself
shall be with them and be their God.
He will wipe every tear from their eyes.
There will be no more death or mourning
or crying or pain, for the old order of things
has passed away.
Revelation 21:3,4

Sometimes we think that by and by
   when we get up to Heav'n
We'll want to ask some questions
   'bout some trials we've been given,
It may be on our heart to ask
   why we have suffered so
And why living wasn't easy
   with its aches and pains, ya' know.

But I have thought on this a tad
   and wondered, could it be
That we'll forget all that bad stuff
   when Jesus face we see?
Our souls will be excited
   when we reach that Golden Shore
And things that used to irk us here
   will bother us no more.

The Bible plainly tells us
   God will wipe away all tears
And He can do that very fast—
   it won't take months or years.
So just be glad and thank the Lord
   when angels give their nod
That you'll leave troubles far behind
   and be at Home with God.

He will wipe every tear from their eyes.

Revelation 21:4

Could It Be?

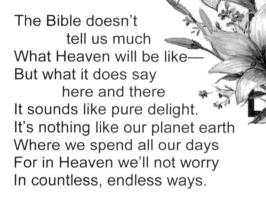

The Bible doesn't
        tell us much
What Heaven will be like—
But what it does say
        here and there
It sounds like pure delight.
It's nothing like our planet earth
Where we spend all our days
For in Heaven we'll not worry
In countless, endless ways.

My husband wondered, "Could it be
Why not too much is said
Is folks might hate to live down here--
Preferring to be dead?"
I hadn't thought of that before,
But I can plainly see
If life is tough and mean down here
We'd like to be set free.

But many folks who live long lives
Enjoy each passing day
And doing things for God and man
Fulfils their lives some way.
I really think God had in mind
That we live here awhile
Then when the angels come for us
We'll greet 'em with a smile.

Not a Millionaire?

I'm really not a millionaire,
But I sure feel like one
  Because God's watching over me,
  And things that He has done.
   But I would like to let you know,
   By naming just a few
    Some blessings that I like a lot
    Though they are old, but true.

    My husband means a lot to me,
    He's gentle and he's kind,
     And having kids who love me, too,
     Gives me a happy mind.
   I also have a lot of friends
   I've gotten here and there
  Although I have a lot of them
  There're none I'd like to spare.

And though I'm blest with lots of things
To feather up my nest
Some things are extra special
And I rate among the best.
To have God's love inside my heart
Along with peace of mind
Tops off my pile of blessings,
But still more things do I find.

When Jesus calls my name down here
I need not moan and groan
Because I know within my heart
I need not go alone.
God's Presence will be with me
When I walk that Golden Stair--
It's then I will discover
That I AM a millionaire!